Cute story and art by
Michael Townsend

cute &

cuter

Alfred A. Knopf
New York

Janie Jane was an expert on all things cute. And on her birthday, she was given the cutest thing she'd ever seen: Sir Yips-a-lot.

From that day on, they were always together.

They were one cute pair.

Fall, winter, spring, summer—each season was cuter than the last.

And before they knew it, it was Janie Jane's birthday again!

Sir Yips-a-lot wasn't so sure about
"The World's Cutest Kitty."

He had always been the cute one in Janie Jane's life. What if she didn't need him anymore?

Sir Yips-a-lot decided he had to do something . . . but what?

His idea: Get Janie Jane's attention and show her he was much cuter than the new kitty.

He began by making all his cutest faces.

But Janie Jane barely noticed.

So he moved on to all his cutest tricks.

Chasing his cute tail . . .

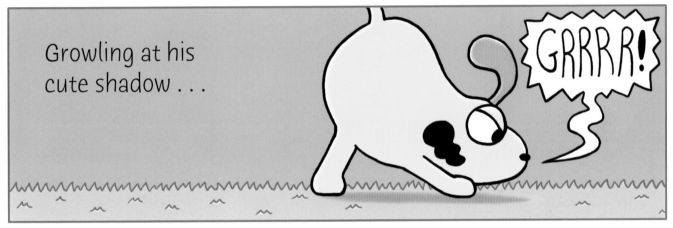

Growling at his cute shadow . . .

And his cute-tastic howling and dancing show . . .

Finally Janie Jane noticed him.

Sir Yips-a-lot began to feel something he had never felt before: **_JEALOUSY!!!_**

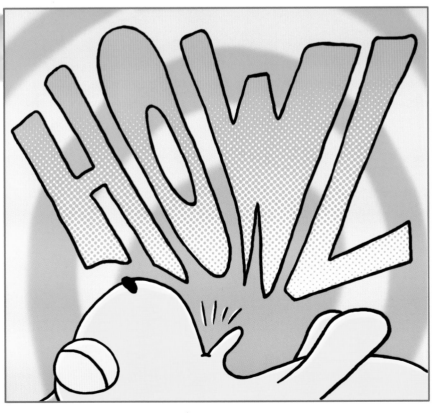

Sir Yips-a-lot spent the rest of the afternoon thinking up ways to get rid of his cute competition.

But Lady Meow-meow was nowhere to be found.
Something terrible might have happened to her.
And it was all his fault!

Suddenly Sir Yips-a-lot heard a cute noise in the distance.

Somehow Lady Meow-meow had fallen into a trash can.
Sir Yips-a-lot sprang into action.

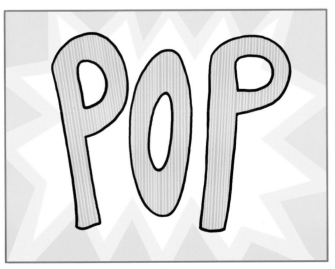

Sir Yips-a-lot was sad. It was clear Janie Jane didn't need cute Sir Yips-a-lot when she had *cuter* Lady Meow-meow.

But before he could slink away into the night, something surprising happened.

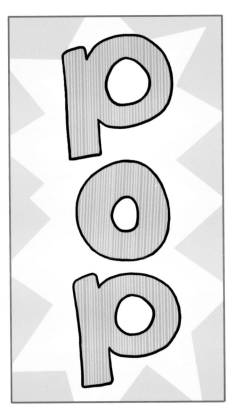

As the long day came to an end, Sir Yips-a-lot realized that Lady Meow-meow wasn't cute competition. She was a new member of the family. And together, they were cuter than ever!

From that day on, the cute trio was inseparable.

Fall, winter, spring, summer—with each season, they grew closer and cuter.

Until Janie Jane's next birthday.

THE END

THIS   IS A

BORZOI BOOK PUBLISHED   BY ALFRED A. KNOPF

Copyright © 2013 by Michael Townsend ♥ All rights reserved. Published in the United States by Alfred A. Knopf, an imprint of Random House Children's Books, a division of Random House, Inc., New York. ♥ Knopf, Borzoi Books, and the colophon are registered trademarks of Random House, Inc. ♥ Visit us on the Web! randomhouse.com/kids ♥ Educators and librarians, for a variety of teaching tools, visit us at RHTeachersLibrarians.com ♥ *Library of Congress Cataloging-in-Publication Data* ♥ Townsend, Michael (Michael Jay). ♥ Cute & cuter / cute story and art by Michael Townsend. — 1st ed. ♥ p. cm. ♥ Summary: Cute pup Sir Yips-a-lot is best friends with his owner Janie Jane, until a cuter new pet comes along and threatens to replace him. ♥ ISBN 978-0-375-85718-8 (trade) — ISBN 978-0-375-95718-5 (lib. bdg.) — ISBN 978-0-307-97448-8 (ebook) ♥ [1. Jealousy—Fiction. 2. Dogs—Fiction. 3. Cats—Fiction. 4. Animals—Infancy—Fiction.] I. Title. II. Title: Cute and cuter. ♥ PZ7.T6639Cut 2013 [E]—dc23 2012026742 ♥ The illustrations in this book were created using black pen and ink and digital coloring. ♥ MANUFACTURED IN MALAYSIA ♥ June 2013 ♥ 10 9 8 7 6 5 4 3 2 1 ♥ First Edition ♥ Random House Children's Books supports the First Amendment and celebrates the right to read.